Bobby Bobcat

Bobby Bobcat

Dave and Pat Sargent

Illustrated by
Blaine Sapaugh

Ozark Publishing, Inc.
P.O. Box 228
Prairie Grove, AR 72753

F
Sar   Sargent, Dave
        Bobby Bobcat, by Dave and Pat Sargent.
Illus. by Blaine Sapaugh.
        Ozark Publishing, Inc., 1996.
        43P. Illus. (Animal Pride Series)
        Summary: After Daddy Bobcat came home,
Bobby grew very fond of him. He even slipped
away from safety to follow him hunting.
        1. Bobcats. I. Sargent, Pat. II. Title. III.
Series.

ISBN Casebound 1-56763-079-0
ISBN Paperback 1-56763-012-X

Ozark Publishing, Inc.
P.O. Box 228
Prairie Grove, AR 72753
Ph: 1-800-321-5671

Printed in the United States Of America

Inspired by

the time when I was twelve years old and riding in the back seat of an old car being driven by my dad. He was driving down a narrow road with high banks on each side. There was a wolf hunt going on, and, all of a sudden, a frightened bobcat almost jumped through the car window. After that, I always kept my car windows rolled up on country roads.

Dedicated to

all children who enjoy watching nature shows on T.V. Kids learn a lot that way.

Foreword

When Daddy Bobcat was finally allowed to come home and help feed and care for the kittens, Bobby grew very fond of him. When Daddy Bobcat went on a hunting trip, Bobby slipped away from his mama and the hollow log and followed. Bobby loved adventure. Things were okay until he decided to try and swim a raging river.

Contents

Bobby Bobcat

One

The Bobtailed Kitten

Mama Dink had just given birth to six little balls of fluffy, soft fur. Their coats were tawny brown, with white under-parts, and numerous black spots over the body. They were the new addition to the bobcat family.

The kittens' eyes were closed at birth. It would be about ten days before they would open. Those first few days were spent drinking Mama Dink's milk and sleeping.

After ten days, the little bob-cats had tripled in size. As their eyes opened, they noticed that they all looked the same.

After their eyes were fully open, Mama Dink named them all. She named five, and as she groomed the last one, she said, "I'm going to call you Bobby."

"Why Bobby?" he asked.

"Because you're special," she replied.

Bobby noticed that all the other kittens could always tell him from the others. What he couldn't figure out was why he couldn't tell them apart.

Mama Dink had made her home in a hollow log. She had

used dry moss and leaves to make her bed. When the kittens were old enough to leave the log, she took them out for a couple of hours each day. It was almost time to wean them.

For the next two weeks, Mama Dink gradually weaned the kittens. She made sure they got plenty of fresh air and exercise. She led them through the brush to the nearby creek so they could watch her catch field mice, hares, and even a porcupine to eat.

Mama Dink often spoke of the kittens' dad. Bobby Bobcat listened when she spoke of his daddy. He wasn't sure what a daddy was, but he figured it was something good.

Mama Dink knew that Bobby's dad was nearby. She had seen him waiting down by the creek. She walked down that way and gave a loud purr. It was the signal they had agreed on. When it was time for him to come home and help with bringing the kittens food, she was to go down to the creek and purr real loud.

Bobby Bobcat was right on his mama's heels. She didn't know that he was following her. When Bobby's dad heard the loud purr, he knew what it meant. He knew that it was time for him to go home. He would now be allowed to play with the kittens and help bring them food. He was excited and let out a loud caterwaul.

The caterwaul scared Bobby half to death! He jumped about six feet into the air, and the hair on his back stood straight up! He whirled in mid-air and hit the ground running. When he reached the hollow log, he crawled inside

and flattened himself on the bed
of dry moss and leaves. He closed
his eyes real tight and waited.

Bobby's brothers and sisters
asked, "What is it, Bobby?
What's wrong? Is a bear after
you?"

Bobby slowly opened his
eyes. He glanced toward the open
end of the log, fully expecting the
caterwaul to come through it.
When nothing appeared, Bobby

got to his feet. He crept to the opening and looked out. There, coming out of the night, was Mama Dink, and walking beside her was a big bobcat. It was the biggest bobcat he had ever seen.

Bobby drew his head back and whispered, "Look, everyone! Look at that big bobcat with Mama."

The kittens rushed to the opening. They all couldn't fit at the same time, so they pushed and shoved each other, trying to get a glimpse of the bobcat.

Mama Dink stopped and they heard her say, "I wonder where the kittens are. They were supposed to wait right here." She called out, "Bobby, you and the others come here. Come see who I've brought home with me. He's been waiting to meet you."

Bobby sat perfectly still. He was not about to go near the big bobcat. He was almost certain that this bobcat was the one who had made the loud caterwauling

sound. And he figured that anything that made a sound that bad
had to be pretty mean!

The kittens pushed their way
past Bobby, who seemed glued to
the floor of the log. They said,
"Ah, come on, Bobby. He won't
hurt you. Let's go see who he is.
Boy! He sure is big!"

All of Bobby's brothers and sisters gathered round Mama Dink and the large bobcat. Mama Dink said, "Children, this is your daddy. He has come home to help feed and care for you. You are to do as he says, for he will be a good teacher."

Daddy Bobcat sniffed each kitten as he circled them. And as he sniffed each one, Mama Dink told him that kitten's name.

When Daddy Bobcat had finished getting acquainted with the five kittens, he counted them, then said, "I thought there were six of you. Where is the other kitten?" He looked all around, but there was not another kitten in sight.

Bobby Bobcat had been watching the other kittens, and saw that they were getting along fine with the new bobcat. He gathered his courage and crawled out of the log.

Daddy Bobcat saw Bobby and said, "There is the sixth kitten. Tell me, Dink, is that one a boy or a girl?"

Mama Dink said, "Oh, that is Bobby. Bobby is our little bob-tailed son. Come over here, Bobby, and meet your daddy."

Bobby walked slowly toward his mama and the others. He stopped in front of his daddy and proudly raised his head.

Daddy Bobcat sniffed Bobby. He walked all around him, checking him out. He noticed Bobby's tail. It was not as long as the other kittens' tails. In fact, it was very, very short. Bobby was a bobtailed bobcat, and Daddy Bobcat said so. He said, "Well, would you look at this one. Bobby is a true bobtailed

bobcat. You'll do fine, son. You'll do just fine."

Bobby said, "Hello, Daddy." He sniffed Daddy Bobcat so that he would know what he smelled like, in case his daddy was gone a lot. Of course, if his daddy let out that caterwaul again, he'd know him for sure. He said, "Daddy, would you teach me how to caterwaul like you?"

Daddy Bobcat laughed and said, "Sure, Bobby. Someday when you are big, like me, you'll be able to caterwaul, too." He looked around at Mama Dink and said, "Tonight we will celebrate. I'll go hunting and bring home something special for supper."

Bobby wanted to go hunting with his dad, but he was afraid to ask. He knew that he was too small to keep up with his daddy's long legs.

Two

The Hunt

Later that night, Daddy
Bobcat left for the hunt.
While he was gone, Mama Dink

told the kittens to wash their paws and groom themselves. That is, she told five of the kittens. It seemed that Bobby was missing.

Bobby Bobcat had followed his dad when his dad had left for the hunt. He hadn't really meant to. He just couldn't help himself. He was keeping up fine until Daddy Bobcat rounded a curve in the narrow trail and disappeared.

Bobby walked around the same curve and was surprised to see nothing but trees. His dad had completely vanished. He was afraid to call out for his dad, for he knew that Daddy Bobcat would scold him for following so deep into the woods.

Bobby turned back. He realized now that he should not have come this far from home. He

stopped and looked all around. He couldn't see far, but he didn't recognize anything. He thought to himself, "Now what am I going to do? How can I survive alone in the woods?"

Bobby walked in the general direction of home. He walked and walked until he grew very tired. He was so tired that he couldn't put one foot in front of the other. He crossed a shallow creek, then saw an old hollow log. He crawled into the log and went to sleep.

Bobby Bobcat didn't know it, but someone was watching out for him. His daddy had known all along that Bobby was following

him. He had deliberately led Bobby
around that curve in the trail, and
then, when Bobby couldn't see, he
had leaped onto the lower limb of
a giant white oak tree.

Daddy Bobcat had sat on the
lower bough of that tree, watching
Bobby, thinking that it was time
for Bobby to learn his first lesson.
He had followed Bobby when he
started home, proud to see that his

son seemed to have a keen sense of direction.

When Daddy Bobcat saw Bobby crawl into the old log, he thought, "That's a fine place to rest, son. Just stay right there until I find us some supper. I'll come by for you when I get ready to go home."

Well, Bobby didn't take a very long nap. His nap was rudely interrupted. There was a wet, wiggly nose in his face. It sniffed up and down his curled-up body. He opened his eyes but stayed perfectly still. To his surprise, he saw a furry, white thing sitting there. It was in the log with him.

Sammy Skunk asked, "Why are you sleeping in my bed, little bobcat? Don't you have a bed of your own?"

Bobby said, "I'm lost. I don't know where my bed is. My name is Bobby Bobcat. What's yours?"

Sammy said, "You know. Everyone knows my name."

Bobby shook his head and said, "I don't. I don't know anyone's name, except for my mama, my daddy, and my brothers and sisters. I know their names."

"Okay. If you don't know my name, I'll tell you. My name is Sammy Skunk."

Sammy waited for Bobby's reaction. When Bobby's expression didn't change, he asked, "Didn't you hear me? I said that I'm a skunk. No one likes me. I don't even have a friend."

Bobby said, "I'll be your friend, Sammy."

"Okay, friend," Sammy said, "move over. There's room for both of us. I'll keep you company for a while, then I'll have to go hunting. I haven't eaten tonight."

Bobby moved over, and Sammy squeezed in beside him. Bobby thought, "Boy, I wish Mama and Daddy and my brothers and sisters could see me now. I have a friend!"

Three

Bobby Swims the River

B obby dozed off again and the next time he opened his eyes, Sammy was gone. He decided that he had rested long enough, so he crawled out of the log and stretched, then started in the direction of home.

There was no moon now. The sky was cloudy, and the moon was hidden behind the clouds. Bobby could not see very well, and he took a wrong turn at the fork in the trail.

Bobby followed the trail for several minutes. Suddenly, there was no more trail. It ended at the edge of a river.

Bobby looked at the river and said, "Boy! That's the biggest creek I ever saw! I don't remember the creek being this big!"

Bobby didn't know much about swimming. His mama had taken the kittens to the creek several times, and had taught them to dog-paddle, as she called it.

He waded into the shallow water. Then, when his feet could no longer touch bottom, he said, "I'll have to swim to the other side. I just know that's where home is."

Well, Bobby started dog-paddling like his mama had taught him. A storm was moving in, and just as he reached the middle of the river, the wind and rain hit.

The smooth water quickly changed to little waves, and

Bobby was being tossed about. He became frightened and let out a loud purring sound. It was something between a purr and a caterwaul.

Back at the old hollow log, Daddy Bobcat stopped by to pick up Bobby. He had found something good for their supper and was ready to go home. When he saw that Bobby wasn't there, he started worrying. "Now where could that little bobtailed bobcat be?" he wondered.

Daddy Bobcat left his catch beside the log and began trailing Bobby. When he reached the fork in the trail, a feeling of fear ran through his body. He knew that Bobby had taken the wrong path, and he knew that it led to the river.

Daddy Bobcat picked up speed. He had almost reached the edge of the river when the storm hit. He said, "This is terrible! I hope Bobby didn't go into the water."

Just then he heard the half-purr, half-caterwaul sound coming from somewhere in the choppy

water. He knew that it must be his little bobtailed son, and he could tell by the cry that Bobby was in trouble.

Daddy Bobcat was a good swimmer, but he didn't like the river. He had only swam across it a time or two, when an old black-and-tan coonhound had been chasing him.

Daddy Bobcat threw back his head and gave his loud caterwaul.

Out in the middle of the choppy water, Bobby Bobcat heard the caterwaul and knew that his dad was near.

With a big leap, Daddy Bobcat landed in the bough of a tree and walked along a limb that grew out over the water. When he reached the end of the limb, he looked down into the river and spotted Bobby.

Daddy Bobcat jumped further than he had ever jumped before. He seemed to sail out over the water. He landed close behind Bobby. He swam to Bobby and, with his powerful jaws, grabbed him by the nape of

the neck. He began swimming
back toward the bank, pulling
Bobby along with him.

When they reached the bank,
they crawled out and shook themselves, slinging water everywhere.
Daddy Bobcat asked, "Are you
okay, Bobby?"

Bobby was so tired, he
couldn't reply. He just lay on the
wet ground thinking how lucky he

was to be alive. Finally he rose to his feet and, with wobbly legs, started slowly toward home. Suddenly he stopped, turned around, and said, "Thank you, Daddy, for rescuing me from the water. That sure is a big creek, isn't it, Daddy?"

Daddy Bobcat smiled and said, "It certainly is, son. Do you mind if I lead the way home? We need to stop by an old log on the way and pick up our supper."

Bobby fell in line behind his dad, thinking, "I'm never going into the woods again. Well, not until I get a little older."

When Daddy Bobcat and Bobby reached home, Mama Dink prepared a fine supper. It was a supper that Bobby would never forget.

Bobby grew into a fine bobcat. He was bigger than his brothers and sisters. He was even bigger than his dad. He weighed a whopping sixty-nine pounds when he was full-grown. And Bobby Bobcat could let out a caterwaul louder than them all.

Bobcat Facts

Abobcat is a medium-sized, bobtailed member of the cat family. It is a relative of the lynx. The bobcat ranges from southern Canada to Mexico. It is differentiated from the lynx by its smaller size, shorter legs, the absence of large, furry foot pads, and by the slightly longer tail marked with black bands only on its upper surface. The ears are more rounded and have less prominent tufts.

An adult male bobcat is thirty-one to thirty-five inches long, including the tail of five to six and a half inches. Its weight is about twenty-two pounds, but exceptionally large males have weighed up to sixty pounds. The female is smaller. The coat is tawny brown, with white underparts, and there are numerous black spots over the body. The forehead, ruff, and legs are striped with black; the backs of the ears are black, with prominent central white spots. The fur is soft and not very durable, but it is sometimes used for sports jackets and coat trimmings.

Bobcats are generally active at night. They are solitary, bold, silent stalkers of small game such as hares, mice, porcupines, and small birds. Occasionally they prey upon deer, young lambs and goats, and poultry, and may make depredations upon poultry, turkey, and sheep ranches. Their eyesight and hearing are good; their sense of smell is of secondary importance.

Bobcats utter a variety of sounds, from loud purrs to cater-wauls. When they run, they have

an ungainly bounding gait, but they can climb well and leap into the lower boughs of trees. They swim only reluctantly, as when they are being chased by hounds in bobcat hunting.

A bobcat's lair is constructed of dry moss or leaves in a hollow log, rock crevice, or thicket, or under a stump. The litter, which contains up to seven kittens, is born any time between late April and early October, after a gestation period of about sixty days. The mother drives off her mate; but later, when the kittens are weaned, she permits him to assist in bringing them food.